MISSION ALERT

ISLAND X

Bloomsbury Education
An imprint of Bloomsbury Publishing Plc

50 Bedford Square	1385 Broadway
London	New York
WC1B 3DP	NY 10018
UK	USA

www.bloomsbury.com

BLOOMSBURY and the Diana logo are trademarks of Bloomsbury Publishing Plc

First published in 2017 by Bloomsbury Education

A catalogue record for this book is available from the British Library.

Library of Congress Cataloguing-in-Publication data has been applied for.

ISBN:	PB:	978-1-4729-2956-3
	ePub:	978-1-4729-2957-0
	ePDF:	978-1-4729-2958-7

2 4 6 8 10 9 7 5 3 1

Typeset by Integra Software Services Pvt. Ltd.

Printed and bound in China by Leo Paper Products

This book is produced using paper that is made from wood grown in managed,
sustainable forests. It is natural, renewable and recyclable. The logging and manufacturing
processes conform to the environmental regulations of the country of origin.

To find out more about our authors and books visit www.bloomsbury.com.
Here you will find extracts, author interviews, details of forthcoming
events and the option to sign up for our newsletters.

recommended by

www.catchup.org

Catchup is a charity which aims to address the problem of underachievement
that has its roots in literacy and numeracy difficulties.

MISSION ALERT
ISLAND X

BENJAMIN HULME-CROSS

Illustrated by
Kanako and Yuzuru

BLOOMSBURY EDUCATION
AN IMPRINT OF BLOOMSBURY

LONDON OXFORD NEW YORK NEW DELHI SYDNEY

Tom and his twin sister Zilla go to a boarding
school. They don't like it very much. But Tom
and Zilla have a secret. They work as spies
for the Secret Service. Sometimes there is a
spy mission that children are better at than
grown-ups. That's when Tom and Zilla get
their next Mission Alert!

CONTENTS

Chapter One

Zilla and Tom were playing football with some friends. Suddenly Zilla stopped running. Her watch was buzzing. She looked across at Tom.

She could tell that his watch was buzzing too. That could mean only one thing. The Secret Service had a new mission for them!

Zilla pretended that she had hurt her leg. Tom ran over to help Zilla off the field.

They sat down under a tree where no one could see them and then they plugged earphones into their watches.

The watches had lots of special spy features. The Secret Service could find Zilla and Tom at any time by tracking their watches.

They tapped the screens and the instructions began.

"Agents, here is your next mission," they heard Marcus say. Marcus was their handler at the Secret Service.

"There is a firm called Starcorp," he said.

"They make satellites and lots of other high tech stuff. The owner of Starcorp is the billionaire, Boris Silver," Marcus explained.

Tom and Zilla knew the name Silver. There was a boy in their class called Jake Silver. Boris Silver was his dad. Tom and Zilla didn't like Jake. Not many people did. He was the sort of kid who showed off because his dad was rich.

"Boris Silver owns an island," said Marcus.

Everyone at school knew that Jake Silver's dad owned an island. Jake was always showing off about it.

"We have been spying on Boris Silver," said Marcus, "He has built a second island next to the first."

Jake and Zilla saw some pictures on their watch screens.

They were photos of the islands, taken from the sky.

"We are calling this new island 'Island X'," explained Marcus.

"Look closely at the round building on Island X. Silver says that this is where he is developing a super-powerful telescope."

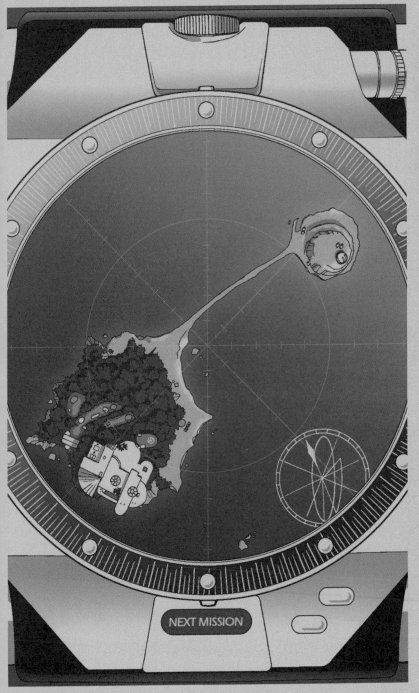

NEXT MISSION

Tom and Zilla saw more pictures on their watch screens. One picture showed a round building with an area of the roof pulled back.

"The Secret Service is worried," explained Marcus, "because when our satellites fly over the islands we lose contact with them."

"So you think that Silver is using his telescope to jam the signal from our satellites?" asked Tom.

"But why would he do that?" said Zilla.

"Boris Silver makes and sells satellites," said Marcus.

"But the government has never bought any of his satellites. We don't trust him. We think he is trying to stop our satellites from working properly so that we will be forced to buy his. It's all about money," Marcus said.

"OK. So you want us to find out what is happening on Island X," said Zilla.

"That's right," said Marcus. "Good luck!"

Chapter Two

Zilla and Tom had a plan. They decided they would pretend to be best friends with Jake Silver. Then he would invite them to visit his dad's island.

They sat next to him at dinner. They cheered him on at football. They even laughed at his jokes. Jake wasn't used to having any friends because he showed off so much. He was so happy he invited Zilla and Tom to visit his dad's island.

So at half term, Zilla, Tom and Jake went to Boris Silver's island. They flew in Boris Silver's private helicopter. As they were about to land they looked down and saw Island X for the first time.

"See?" shouted Jake. "I told you this would be amazing. I bet you've never done anything this cool!"

Tom and Zilla looked at each other. Jake was showing off again but they didn't say anything.

The helicopter landed and Jake led Tom and Zilla towards a very grand house. A huge man opened the door. He was wearing very smart clothes but he looked like a thug. He stared hard at Tom and Zilla.

"Get out of our way," Jake shouted rudely at the man. "I'll show Tom and Zilla around the house. You get our bags from the helicopter!"

The man looked very cross at being told what to do by a boy, but he just said, "Very good, Sir."

"That's Simpson, our butler," said Jake. "He has to do what I tell him."

Tom and Zilla looked at each other but they didn't say anything.

"Hey Jake, can we explore the island first?" Tom asked. "This place is epic!"

"OK," said Jake. He was pleased that Tom and Zilla thought his dad's island was amazing.

As they set off to explore the island they saw the helicopter taking off. Simpson was looking up at it and shouting into a walkie-talkie.

The island was quite small and it only took them about half an hour to walk around it.

When they came to the point where they could see Island X, Tom began asking questions. Jake told them that his dad had built Island X as a place where Starcorp could test telescopes.

"But why did he need to build an island?" Tom wanted to know. "Why not just buy a field or something?"

"Oh, stop asking so many questions!" Jake said crossly. "If my dad wants to build an island, he builds an island. And I'm going to be just like him when I grow up."

Zilla looked across at Island X. She could see one side of the round building. And on top of the wall she could see guards.

It looked like they were holding weapons.

Zilla saw that the guards were pointing at her...

Chapter Three

Jake's room was full of very expensive things.

There were games consoles. There was a huge TV.

There was even a drone in one corner of the room.

"You've got to see this game." Jake said, giving them both handsets. "My dad bought it for me and it's not even out yet. Nobody else has it."

They sat down on giant bean bags and began playing Jake's new game. The rest of the day was the same. Jake showed off about his amazing life.

He was rude to Simpson the butler. He bossed Tom and Zilla around. Tom and Zilla let him win the new game. They were getting really fed up when the door to Jake's room burst open.

"Dad!" said Jake. He didn't sound happy. He sounded scared.

Boris Silver did not even look at Jake.

He stared at Tom and then Zilla. "Who are you?" he asked crossly.

"These are my friends I told you about…" Jake began.

"Shut up!" Boris shouted. "You don't have friends because nobody likes you."

He turned to Zilla. "Why are you really here?" he asked.

Zilla felt really scared but she also felt angry. Why was Boris Silver so horrible to Jake?

"How can you talk to your own son like that?" Zilla said. "We are here because we **are** Jake's friends. And if you don't want him making friends then don't send him to school!"

Boris stared at Zilla. He looked so angry. But then he turned around and walked out of the room.

"Phew!" said Zilla.

"Is he always like that?" Tom asked.

"Not always," said Jake. He sounded a bit like he might cry. "He's only that angry when something important is going on with his work..."

Chapter Four

Later that night, when everyone was in bed, Zilla's watch began flashing. This was the signal she had agreed with Tom. Time to check out Island X!

She quietly got out of bed, put her clothes on and tip-toed out into the corridor to meet Tom.

They crept downstairs. Every time a floorboard creaked they stopped to listen in case anyone had heard them. Tom led the way towards the large front door.

He was about ten steps away from it when he stopped and held his hand up. Zilla nearly bumped into his back. Suddenly, she saw why he had stopped. Sitting in a chair near the front door was Simpson the butler!

They stayed quite still, waiting for him to jump up and shout at them.

Then, they heard a noise. It was the sound of snoring. Simpson was asleep.

They crept on. The door opened with a soft click. Simpson carried on snoring and Tom and Zilla went outside.

"Now for the hard part!" Zilla whispered.

But she was wrong. Everything went smoothly. They walked over to Island X without any problems.

They could see the outline of the round building.

She stared at the top of the wall, but she couldn't see any guards up there. They heard a noise coming from behind them. They stopped and listened but they heard nothing else.

They began creeping around the edge of the building. At last they came to a small door.

Zilla tapped at her watch and clicked on the lock-pick app. She held the watch against the door where she guessed the lock would be.

The app undid the lock and they heard it click open. Zilla turned the handle, pushed the door open and they both stepped inside.

They were standing on a metal walkway, high up on the side of a large room. The room was huge. It went down deep into the ground.

There were about twenty men and women in white coats at computers around the edge of the room. It was like the inside of a factory. In the middle was a huge machine with a barrel that pointed straight up.

There was a grinding noise. Zilla grabbed Tom's arm and pointed up.

The roof above the machine was slowly opening. Zilla switched her phone to camera mode and began filming.

"It looks like they are about to use it, whatever it is," said Tom.

"British satellite M–I–S 523 coming into range in five minutes!" one of the men called out.

"Ready to send jamming signal!" said another.

"So they **are** trying to mess up the satellites!" Zilla whispered. "Marcus should be getting live video from my watch. The army will be here in a few minutes."

And then they each felt a large hand on their shoulder.

"Gotcha!" said Simpson.

Chapter Five

Simpson led Tom and Zilla down to the huge machine. Boris Silver was standing there. He had a nasty smile on his face.

"I **knew** you were here to cause trouble!" said Boris Silver. "Of course, I won't be able to let you go now. You've seen too much."

"Did you really think there weren't any guards on duty tonight? I knew you wanted to see inside these secret buildings and I wanted to catch you in the act!" Silver laughed.

"And what did you catch us doing?" Zilla asked. "We were just having a look around."

"YOU ARE SPIES!" Silver shouted. "But you are **not** going to stop me. I am going to see to it that every object in space is owned by Starcorp. And two kids are not going to get in my way!"

"That's where you are wrong," said Tom.
"We have been recording everything you've
been saying."

Zilla held up her watch.

Boris Silver looked so angry Tom thought he might burst. Suddenly, there was a shout and the sound of lots of boots on the metal staircase. The soldiers Zilla had called had arrived.

* * *

A short while later Tom and Zilla stood on the lawn outside the main house. Jake was with them. The soldiers had woken him up. Two men led Boris Silver across the lawn towards an army helicopter. He was in handcuffs and he shouted at the soldiers all the way to the helicopter.

"Sorry about your dad, Jake," said Tom.

"It's OK," said Jake quietly. "Home is going to be a better place without him around."

Bonus Bits!

Guess Who?

Each of the quotes below comes from one of these characters in the story:

1 Zilla

2 Tom

3 Marcus

4 Jake

5 Boris

Match the character to the quote by writing down the correct letter next to the number. Check your answers at the end of this section (no peeking!).

a "Oh, stop asking so many questions!"

b "It looks like they are about to use it, whatever it is."

c "You don't have friends because nobody likes you."

d "Agents, here is your next mission."

e "How can you talk to your own son like that?"

Great Gadget!

Zilla and Tom have some very cool watches in their role helping the Secret Service. Look at the list of watch features below and write down the letters of the ones that are used during their Island X mission:

a they buzz to alert the children to a new mission

b you can plug earphones into them

c you can send a fax from them

d they have a tracking device built in

e you can watch a movie on them when flying on a plane

f they can display photos of important places that are part of the mission before the children go on the mission

g they change colour

h they contain a lock–pick app

i they can film things the children see

j they show the temperature in a building.

What Next?

- Would you like to do secret missions like Zilla and Tom? Why or why not?
- Even though Jake's dad has lots of money and Jake has lots of things, he is not happy. What does Jake want his dad to do differently?
- Do you think Zilla and Tom will still be friends with Jake after the mission? Give reasons for your answer based on events in the story.
- Design your own gadget that could be used on a spy mission. Think about what features it would need to have and how

these could be hidden from potential enemies. Draw a picture of your design and add labels to show all the features.

ANSWERS to GUESS WHO
1e, 2b, 3d, 4a, 5c

ANSWERS to GREAT GADGET!
The features used in this mission are: a, b, d, f, h, i.

Look out for Tom and Zilla's next spy mission!

ISBN 978-1-4729-2960-0

Turn the page for a sneak preview!

Chapter 2

The next day, Tom and Zilla were outside the entrance to Wonder World Theme Park. They were at the front of the queue.

"This has to be the best mission ever!" said Tom. "Have you got the tickets yet?"

Zilla checked her watch. The Secret Service had said they would email her their entrance tickets.

"Yes, I've got them," said Zilla. "Just in time!" A woman was opening up the kiosk, to let people in to the park. Tom and Zilla showed her their tickets.

Just in front of them were three people dressed up in panda outfits. They were waving at everyone as they came into the park.

"That must be a really weird job!" said Tom.